CELL BLOCK Z

CELL BLOCK Z

CONCEPT BY *GHOSTFACE KILLAH*
SCRIPT BY *SHAUNA GARR*
AND *MARLON CHAPMAN*
ART PRODUCTION BY *5R MEDIA*
ART DIRECTION, DIGITAL INKS,
FINISHES BY *CHRIS WALKER*
LAYOUTS, BREAKDOWNS,
LETTERS BY *ROB HAYNES*
PRODUCTION ASSISTANCE BY *JAMEEL NEWKIRK,*
CHUCK COLLINS, STEVEN VALDEZ

GRAND CENTRAL
PUBLISHING

Grand Central Publishing
Hachette Book Group
237 Park Avenue
New York, NY 10017

Visit our website at www.HachetteBookGroup.com.

Printed in the United States of America

First Edition: July 2009
10 9 8 7 6 5 4 3 2 1

Grand Central Publishing is a division of Hachette Book Group, Inc.
The Grand Central Publishing name and logo is a trademark of Hachette Book Group, Inc.

LCCN: 2009929132
ISBN: 978-0-446-69974-7

CELL BLOCK Z

OUR OWN SONS AND DAUGHTERS HAVE BECOME THE 21ST CENTURY ENEMY, STRONGER, SMARTER, AND WORST OF ALL, HEARTLESS.

YEARS OF DENIAL HAVE PREVENTED US FROM TRACKING AND ELIMINATING TERRORIST CELLS. OUR LAW ENFORCEMENT AND MILITARY ARE ILL-EQUIPPED AND UNPREPARED TO STRIKE WITH THE RELENTLESS VENGEANCE NECESSARY.

THEY SAY I MURDERED SOME SECURITY GUARD AT AIDES FEDERAL AFTER I ROBBED IT.

I WOULDN'T SIGN A CONFESSION, SO THEY TOOK ME TO TRIAL.

I WAS AT MY PLACE GETTING DRESSED WHEN THE ROBBERY TOOK PLACE, SO LET'S SEE THEM PIN THIS SHIT ON ME.

WITNESS AFTER WITNESS ALL SAY THEY SAW ME AT THE SCENE. WHAT ROBBER DOESN'T WEAR A MASK?

THEY EVEN GOT TAPE OF A GUY THAT DAMN SURE LOOKS LIKE ME AT THE SCENE.

VIDEO TIMESTAMP: 02:03

LIFE WITHOUT THE POSSIBILITY OF PAROLE.

BUT NOT JUST LIFE. LIFE AT CAUCASUS PENITENTIARY.

CAUCASUS IS THE MODERN-DAY ALCATRA. IT HOLDS THE WORS OF THE WORST.

COME ON, BABY.
THIS AIN'T NUTHIN'.

PRELIMINARY
FIGHT, MY ASS...

YOU'RE
GOIN' DOWN,
DENNIS.

LET'S SEE
THAT RIGHT OF
YOURS TAKE DOWN
VICTORIUS.

LET'S SEE HOW YOUR HOT PROSPECT
DOES IN A REAL FIGHT. SAY,
FIVE-TO-ONE ODDS.

WHAT IS
THIS?

INMATES FIGHTING EACH
OTHER? THAT'S STRICTLY
PROHIBITED. NOT TO
MENTION INHUMANE.

YOU'RE
ON.

A WAY
FOR PRISONERS
TO RELEASE THEIR
STRESS.

HA-HA.
REMEMBER WHAT I TOLD YA, JOHNSON?
THIS PLACE AIN'T LIKE OTHER PRISONS.

GENTLEMEN AND
GENTLEMEN, TONIGHT
ONE OF OUR TOP FIGHTERS,
VICTORIOUS, TAKES ON
A NEWCOMER.
UH, NO NAME.

FIGHT!

27

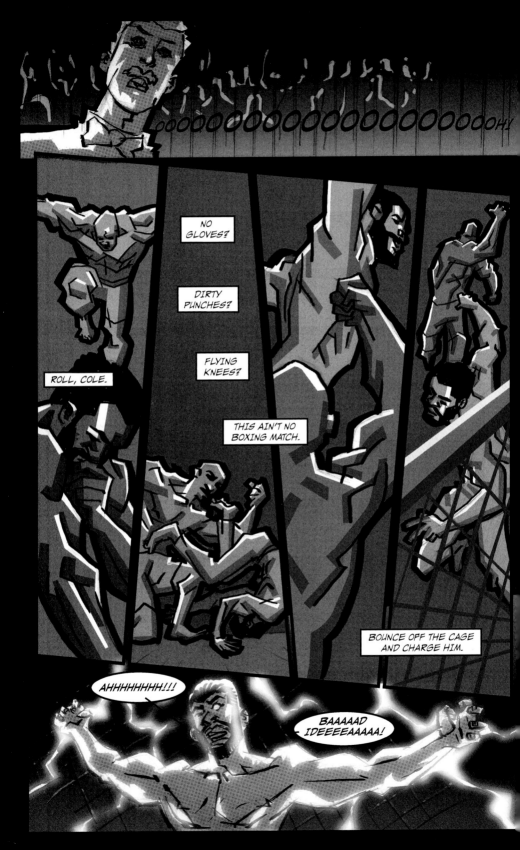

I AM MAN LABELED A MURDERER,
A MAN WITH HIS IDENTITY STOLEN.
A MAN WITH NO FACE. I AM
GHOSTFACE KILLAH.

BUT HE TURNED IT INTO AN OPPORTUNITY TO TRANSFORM, TO BECOME SOMETHING GREATER THAN HIMSELF.

HE CHOSE TO LIBERATE THE WICKED, NOT BECOME ONE OF THEM.

YOU CAN TAKE A STAND AND NOT FIGHT TONIGHT.

HELP ME FIGURE OUT SOMETHING, JOHNSON?

YOU'VE BEEN COMING TO ME AND THE OTHER INMATES FOR THE PAST YEAR TALKING ABOUT MAKING A DIFFERENCE, TAKING A STAND...

...AND FOR THAT SAME YEAR, I'VE BEEN WATCHING YOU HIDE BEHIND THAT BIBLE, HELPING RECEIVE SHIPMENTS OF WHO-KNOWS-WHAT LATE AT NIGHT.

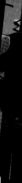

INMATE DENNIS, IT'S NOT THAT SIMPLE.

OH YEAH? YOU KNOW JUST AS WELL AS I DO, THERE'S SOMETHING GOING ON HERE THAT DOESN'T GO ON IN ANY OTHER PRISON.

AND ME REFUSING TO FIGHT AIN'T GONNA CHANGE THAT. BUT IT'S MY ONLY SHOT AT GETTING OUTTA THIS NIGHTMARE.

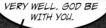

VERY WELL. GOD BE WITH YOU.

I HAVE NEVER BEEN SO HUMILIATED. AND WHAT MAKES IT WORSE IS...

...HE'S RIGHT.

44

INMATE DENNIS, I'VE GOT SOMETHING TO SHOW YOU.

IT'S A COPY OF THE CELL BLOCK Z FILE.

I TOOK IT FROM THE WARDEN'S OFFICE.

OH YEAH?

I'M NOT GONNA ASK WHERE YOU HAD THIS HID.

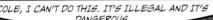

COLE, I CAN'T DO THIS. IT'S ILLEGAL AND IT'S DANGEROUS.

WE'VE BEEN RUNNING IN CIRCLES FOR A YEAR NOW. SOMETHING'S GOTTA GIVE. JUST SEE WHAT'S ON IT.

IT'S PROBABLY GOT A MONSTER SECURITY SYSTEM ON IT, AND A TRACER TO TRACK WHENEVER IT'S READ.

I'M SURE YOU CAN GET AROUND THAT. THIS IS PROOF OF SOMETHING. I DON'T KNOW WHAT, BUT MAYBE IT CAN HELP ME AND OTHER INNOCENT PEOPLE IN HERE.

GIVE IT A LOOK. PLEASE, KAYLA.

OKAY, JUST A LOOK. I GOT A GUY WHO MIGHT BE ABLE TO CRACK IT.

TELL YOUR GUY JOHNSON TO MEET ME ON THE OUTSIDE; I'LL GET IT FROM HIM THEN.

TAKE CARE OF YOURSELF, COLE.

SO THIS IS THE HOLE.

I MUST BE STILL WOOZY. THE GROUND FEELS LIKE IT'S MOVING.

OR IT'S JUST MY NEW CELLMATES...

HE'S INSUBORDINATE. TOTALLY RECKLESS. THESE ARE NOT THE TRAITS OF SOMEONE I WANT. I MOVE TO DROP HIM FROM THE PROGRAM.

I'VE GIVEN HIM SO MUCH TRAINING, HE SHOULDN'T BE THROWN AWAY.

HE NEEDS HOPE. I'LL TALK TO HIM. MAKE HIM FEEL LIKE SOMEONE CARES.

57

WHISPERED CONVERSATIONS.

CRATES WITH BLACK EAGLES ON THEM.

MEN IN LAB COATS BEING HURRIED IN AND OUT OF THE PRISON.

WHAT I **HAVEN'T** SEEN OR HEARD IS ANYONE COME IN OR OUT OF CELL BLOCK Z.

CELL BLOCK Z

KAYLA SAYS SHE'S WORKING ON CRACKING THE DISK. I JUST HOPE SHE DOES IT IN TIME....

I CAN ONLY PROGRAM IT TO REPLICATE ITSELF AS AN INDEPENDENT FILE.

THE PROGRAM KNOWS WHAT I'M DOING... IT'S EATING THE INFORMATION.

TRACE ABORTED.

WHAT THE HELL HAVE YOU GOTTEN ME INTO, KAYLA?

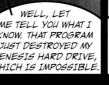

I DON'T KNOW.

WELL, LET ME TELL YOU WHAT I KNOW. THAT PROGRAM JUST DESTROYED MY GENESIS HARD DRIVE, WHICH IS IMPOSSIBLE.

WHATEVER IS ON THIS DISK IS ENOUGH TO GET ME SENT TO CAUCASUS. AND I DON'T WANNA LOSE MY VIRGINITY THERE.

SORRY, WIZ. I'VE GOT YOUR BACK IF THERE'S TROUBLE.

ΣΤΡΑΝΓΕ ΧΟΔΕ
ΣΤΡΑΝΓΕ ΧΟΔΕ
ΣΤΡΑΝΓΕ ΧΟΔΕ
ΣΤΡΑΝΓΕ ....

I'M THE ONE WHO'S SORRY. I WANTED TO SEE WHAT WAS ON THAT DISK.

THAT'S ALL THAT'S LEFT OF THE DISK.

CAN YOU DECODE IT?

WHY DO YOU THINK THEY CALL ME WIZARD?

WHOEVER YOU'RE DOING THIS FOR MUST BE REAL IMPORTANT.

I THINK HE IS.

THANKS FOR EVERYTHING. LET ME KNOW WHEN YOU'VE GOT SOMETHING.

ONE STEP CLOSER, BABY. ONE STEP CLOSER.

61

GREY TOLD ME THE LAST TIME THEY EXECUTED AN ORDER ELEVEN WAS WHEN COLLABORATORS IN THE ASSASSINATION OF PRESIDENT REDDING WERE BELIEVED TO BE IN CAUCASUS.

ALL INMATES HAVE TO STAY IN THE YARD. WE ALL HAVE TO EAT, SLEEP, EVEN SHIT OUTSIDE.

OFFICER JOHNSON
HARRY SEWARD
COLE DENNIS # 46664

WORD IS, THE WARDEN HAS A LIST OF PEOPLE HE WANTS QUESTIONED.

THEY WANTED ME TO GIVE UP JOHNSON. AS BRAUM WHIPPED MY BACK RAW, SOMETIMES I COULD SEE DRAGON SMILING, LIKE HE WAS HAPPY I WOULDN'T BREAK.

THEY'VE BEEN "QUESTIONING" ME ABOUT THE DISK FOR THREE DAYS STRAIGHT. BUT I JUST KEEP THINKING OF KAYLA--THE WAY SHE CARES. THE WAY SHE LOOKS. SILLY AS IT IS, THAT'S WHAT KEEPING ME GOING.

GREY TOLD ME THEY QUESTIONED JOHNSON, TOO. I CRACKED THE FIRST SMILE SINCE I GOT IN HERE WHEN I HEARD HE DIDN'T SNITCH.

WHY CAN'T I STOP THINKING ABOUT HIM?

IT'S NOT PROFESSIONAL.

MAYBE IT'S BECAUSE I'M LONELY. MAYBE I JUST NEED TO GET LAID. MAYBE IT'S BECAUSE I BELIEVE HIM.

LISTEN TO YOU. HE COULD BE A THEIVING, LYING MURDERER FOR ALL YOU KNOW.

KAYLA REESE.

I CRACKED THE DISK. YOU SHOULD COME BY. I'LL LIGHT SOME CANDLES AND WARM UP SOME PIZZA.

I'LL BE RIGHT THERE. NO CANDLES NEEDED.

BUZZZZZ, BUZZZZ...

IT TOOK LONGER THAN NORMAL. I HAD TO CREATE A PROGRAM TO CONVERT IT TO BINARY AND THEN DECODE IT FROM THERE.

SO WHAT IS IT?

IT'S JUST NAMES AND NUMBERS OF INMATES. I CHECKED THEM ALL OUT. THEY ARE ALL CURRENTLY SERVING TERMS AT CAUCASUS IN CELL BLOCK Z.

LOOKS LIKE ROLL CALL TO ME.

LET ME CHECK IT OUT, MIGHT BE SOMETHING IN HERE.

WHAT, NO KISS?

HOW 'BOUT A RAIN CHECK? THANKS A MILLION.

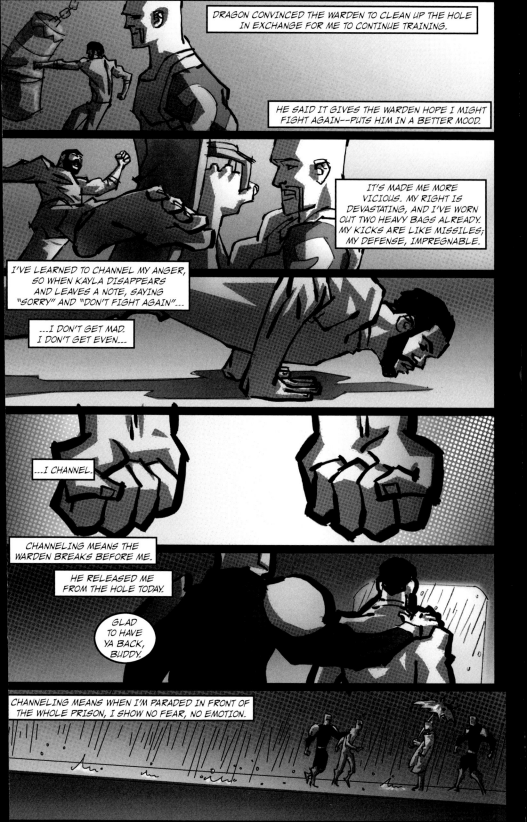

71

STOP!!!

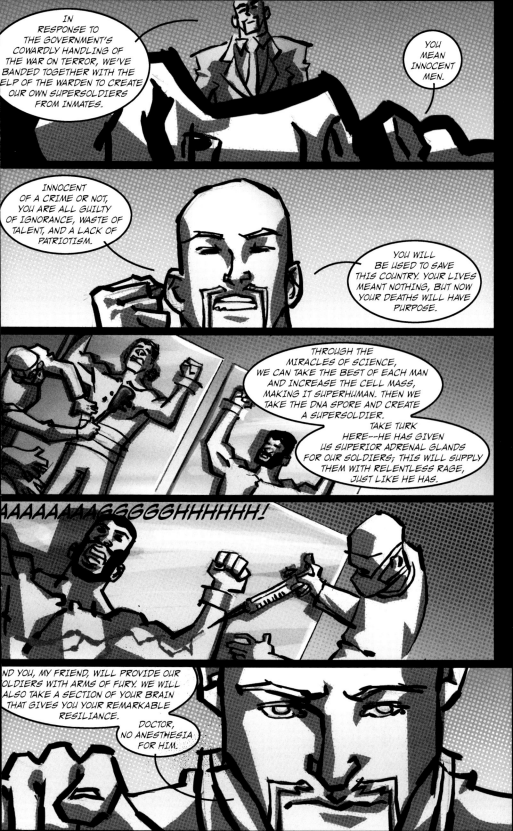

SHIT!
LOOK--IT'S GHOSTFACE!

HE'S IN THE CONTROL TOWER.

SET US FREE, GHOST!

GHOST-FACE ! GHOST-FACE! GHOST-FACE.

THIS IS GOVERNOR RAWLINGS. I HAVE RECEIVED NOTIFICATON...

EVERY AVAILIBLE MAN IS ON HIS WAY. WHAT'S THE STATUS AT THE PRISON?

AFTER ALL THE EXCITEMENT...

NAS +86
DOW +187

CONGRESSIONAL HEARING: CAUCASUS FEDERAL PRISON

ATTORNEY FOR THE PEOPLE
KAYLA REESE
CLEARS 100TH CAUCASUS INMATE.

...IT WAS GOOD TO BE HOME AND WATCH THINGS WORK OUT THE WAY THEY SHOULD.

BUT IT DIDN'T TAKE LONG...

SECURITY CAMERA

AREA: 5
PRISONER TRANSFER

...FOR ME TO SIGN UP FOR MORE TROUBLE.

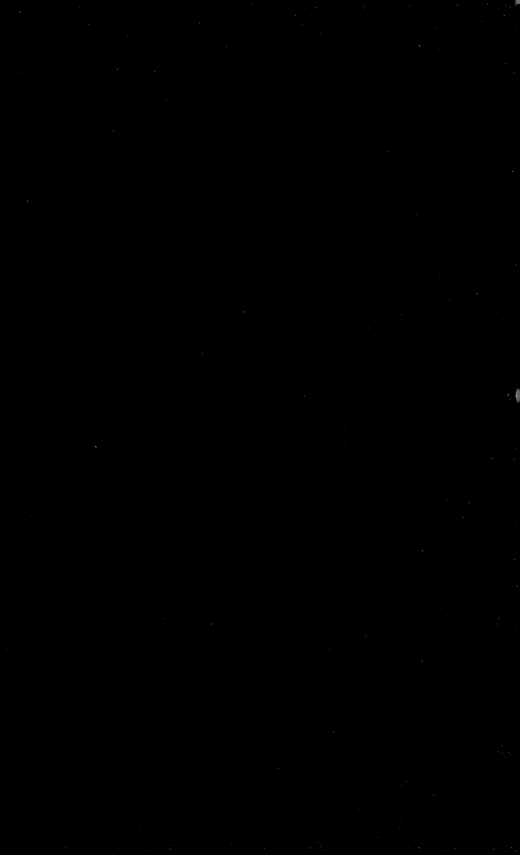